I want to tell you a story about a cat.

Just an ordinary cat,

until the day it did an extraordinary thing.

CAROUSEL CAT

ROBERT J. BLAKE

PHILOMEL BOOKS

Every morning Dan unlocked the doors of the Pavilion O' Fun. And every morning the cat was inside waiting for him. Dan always wondered how the cat got in the building before he did.

But the cat never offered any clues.

Every morning the cat helped Dan inspect and polish the carousel. Then they climbed into the front seat of carriage number three to wait for their friends Madam Fortune and The World's Strongest Tattooed Man.

After saying "Good morning" and "How are you," Madam Fortune and

The World's Strongest Tattooed Man took the controls and sent Dan and the cat around for their own private ride. After a few times around, Dan took over the controls.

They did the same thing, the same way, day after day.

Until someone opened a new amusement park called Scaryland. It had the Sooper Dooper Looper and the Gonna Getcha Gremlin rides. It was bigger and wilder than the old Pavilion O' Fun.

Soon, the owner, Mr. Darnett, said, "There is not enough business. I must close the Pavilion O' Fun."

Fewer and fewer people came to the boardwalk. Mrs. Custard closed Custard's Last Stand. Mr. Hazzard sold off his bumper cars. Before long, Mr. Tony's Char-Broil was the only place still open. And if it weren't for Dan and his friends, Mr. Tony wouldn't have had any business at all.

"I wish we could sit on the carousel just one more time," said Dan.

"The future sits heavily upon us," said Madam Fortune in her mystic voice.

"This sittin' around is making all of us heavy," said The World's Strongest Tattooed Man. "Even the cat is getting pudgy."

Things were different, yet every day was the same. Dan and the cat always met their friends at Mr. Tony's for breakfast. And they met for lunch and for dinner, too. There wasn't much else to do.

But one day, Mr. Tony announced, "I am sorry, but I must close the Char-Broil. Maybe I can open again in the spring."

Madam Fortune and The World's Strongest Tattooed Man started to spend their weekdays looking for jobs.

Now only Dan and the carousel cat met on the boardwalk every morning. They'd slowly walk out to the end of the pier, put a quarter into the Miracle Binoculars and look back at the boardwalk.

"Look, cat," Dan would say. "That's where Hazzard's Bumper Cars used to be." But now there was nothing but boarded-up buildings.

They always ended their day in front of the Pavilion O' Fun.

"I wish we could run the carousel just one more time," Dan always said. Then he'd shake his head, blow his nose, and they'd part ways for the night.

But one morning, the cat did not come. Dan looked in the garbage cans and all its favorite places. But he found no cat.

On Saturday, The World's Strongest Tattooed Man went with him to search. He was a handy helper because he would lift cars and lifeboats so that Dan could see under them. But they found no cat.

On Sunday, Madam Fortune joined the hunt. She was famous for finding things, but even she found no cat.

Dan was about to give up.

Then one day, after a lonely lunch, Dan walked out to the end of the pier and put a coin into the Miracle Binoculars.

And he saw something terrible!

Mr. Tony's Char-Broil was on fire!

Soon there were firemen and policemen and lots of smoke. Many people were pushing and shoving to get a look. And then Dan saw—he thought he saw—yes, he definitely saw the carousel cat!

It ran in and out of people's legs and dashed through an opening in Mr. Tony's door.

Dan hurried down the pier and found his friends Madam Fortune and The World's Strongest Tattooed Man.

"I saw the cat going in and out of the fire!" Dan said.

"I saw him carrying rags or something," said The World's Strongest Tattooed Man to his friend.

"I see the cat right now!" said Madam Fortune, looking at the rooftops.

The cat paced back and forth, then in circles. It disappeared for a moment and then reappeared at the corner of the building.

Madam Fortune closed her eyes and pointed at the Pavilion.

"We must go inside the Pavilion O' Fun," she said in her mystic voice.

"But it's locked," said Dan, "and Mr. Darnett took the keys."

"This requires a feat of strength!" said The World's Strongest Tattooed Man.

The World's Strongest Tattooed Man performed his feat of strength and the three friends went inside.

Madam Fortune put her hand to her head. "There is something under carriage number three," she said.

"Be careful," said Dan.

They walked slowly over to the carriage.

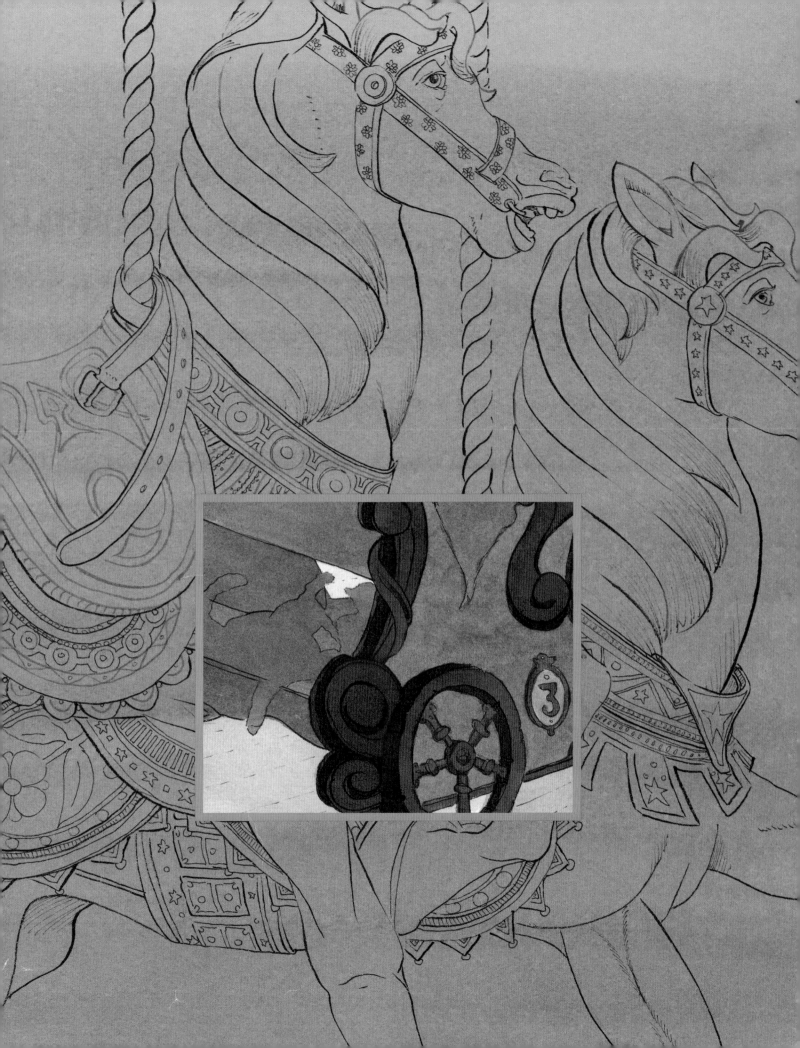

"He's got babies!" said The World's Strongest Tattooed Man.
"Kittens," said Madam Fortune in her normal voice. "*She* has kittens!"
But where was the carousel cat?

They all looked at one another.
Then they all looked up together.
"And there she is with another kitten!"

Way up high, the carousel cat stepped in through a broken window. She had one last kitten in her mouth.

The carousel cat dropped onto a crossbeam. She hurried along the edge and then jumped to a light that hung over the carousel.

But she slipped.

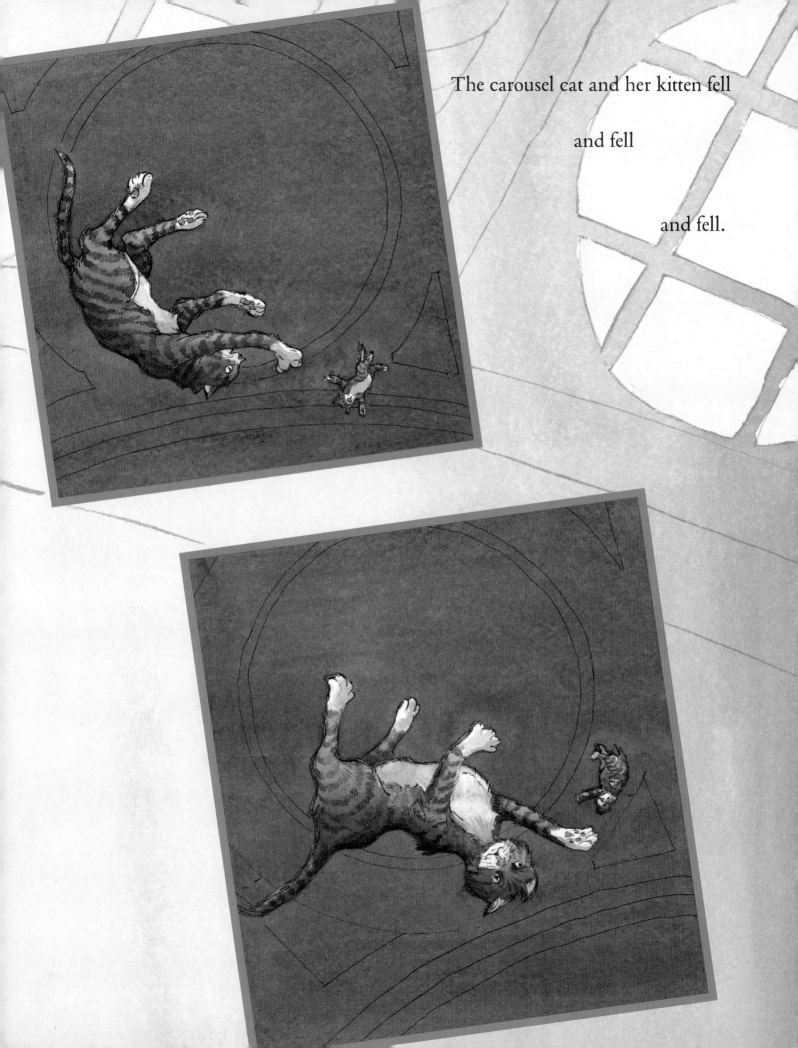

The carousel cat and her kitten fell

and fell

and fell.

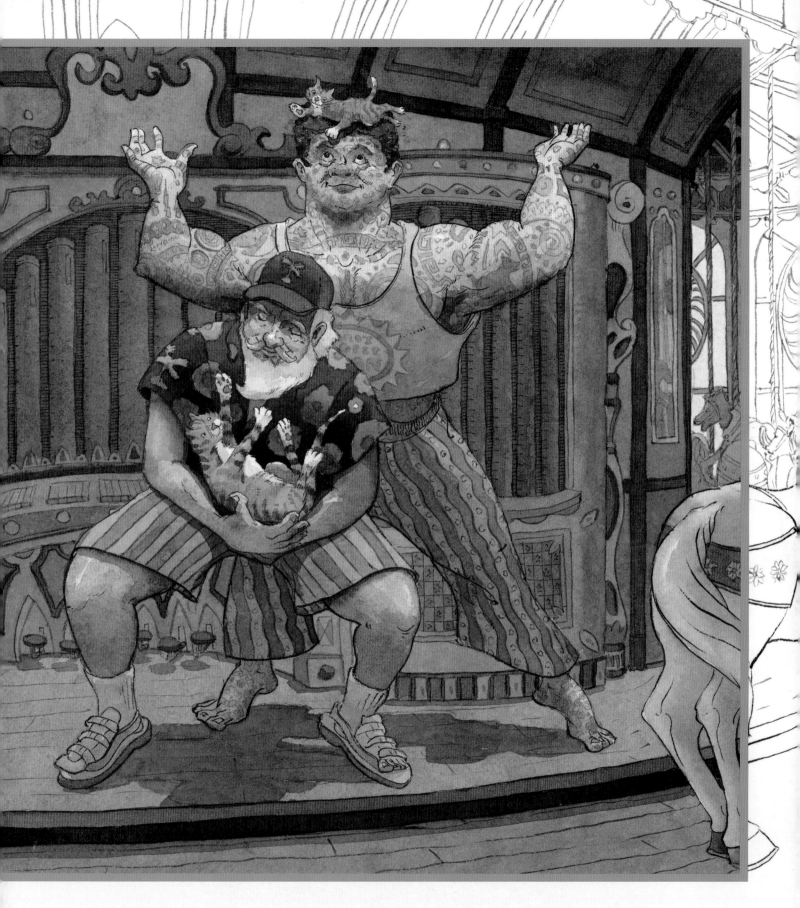

Only to be saved by the daring moves of Dan and The World's Strongest Tattooed Man.

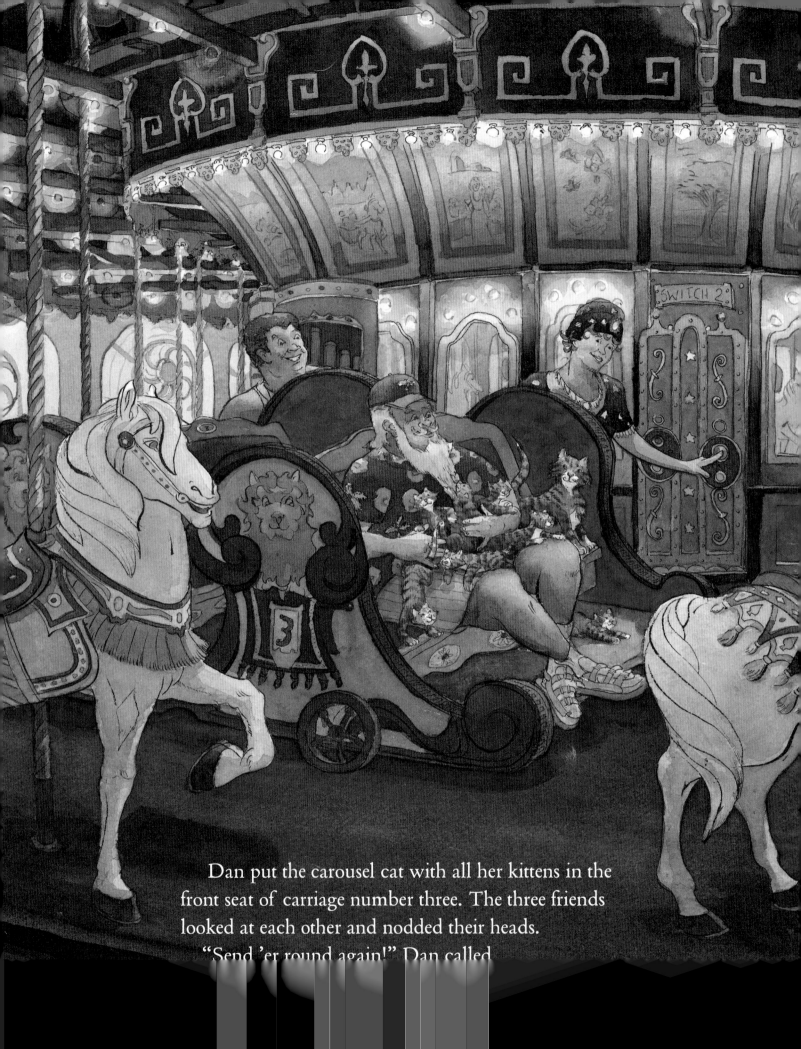

Dan put the carousel cat with all her kittens in the front seat of carriage number three. The three friends looked at each other and nodded their heads.

"Send 'er round again!" Dan called.

And once again, Dan and the carousel cat took their own private ride on the

In memory of Jeanne Waybright, a very special person

AUTHOR'S NOTE

The artwork for *Carousel Cat* was created with ink and watercolor. Most of the preliminary
drawings were done on location in Asbury Park, New Jersey.
I would like to thank Candice Procasini, Tony DiLeo and Bob Bolmer. An extra special
thanks goes out to the Gillians who run one fine carousel in Ocean City, New Jersey.
There's nothing like the Jersey Shore!

PATRICIA LEE GAUCH, EDITOR

Copyright © 2005 by Robert J. Blake

MAY 0 6 2005

PHILOMEL BOOKS,
a division of Penguin Young Readers Group, 345 Hudson Street, New York, NY 10014.
Published simultaneously in Canada. Manufactured in China by South China Printing Co. Ltd.
Designed by Semadar Megged. Text set in 17-point Poliphilus. The art was done in transparent watercolor and ink.
Library of Congress Cataloging-in-Publication Data
Blake, Robert J.
Carousel cat / Robert J. Blake. p. cm. Summary: One day, after Dan is forced to close the boardwalk carousel, he
and his neighbors search for their missing cat friend at the same time that a local building catches fire.
[1. Cats—Fiction. 2. Merry-go-round—Fiction. 3. Beaches—Fiction. 4. Fires—Fiction.] I. Title.
PZ7.B564Car 2005 [E]—dc22 2004006736
ISBN 0-399-23382-2
1 3 5 7 9 10 8 6 4 2
First Impression